♪ BOOGIE ♪ MONSTER

by **Josie Bissett**

illustrated by **Kevan J. Atteberry**

COMPENDIUM
kids

inspiring possibilities

When I was a little girl, my mom or dad would turn on the radio, take me in their arms and swoop me around the room to the music. At weddings, my grandpa would have me stand on his shoes for the slow dances, and my aunts and uncles would pull me out on the floor to "boogie" with them to the fast ones. Everyone needs and deserves Boogie Monsters in their lives—loving, toe-tapping parents, grandparents, or caregivers who can share the joy of music, dance, healthy movement and self-expression with a child. I thank each and every one of you for giving your children these wonderful gifts through this book.
—*Josie Bissett*

Special thanks to **Kobi Yamada** and the entire team at **Compendium**. I am so blessed to get to work with such a talented and inspiring gang! To **Dan Zadra** for your outstanding way with words, I adore you. To **Meredith Clark** for your extraordinary gift of writing and editing, I am so grateful to have the opportunity to work with you. To **Kevan Atteberry**, a monstrous thanks: your passion and illustrations for Tickle Monster and Boogie Monster are simply wonderful. To **Sarah Forster**, **Jessica Phoenix** and **Joanna Price**, a huge thanks for your tireless and invaluable artistic contributions to this book. To **Tote Yamada**, many many thanks for all your special deliveries! To **Recess Monkey**, thank you for the Boogie Monster music you created; you guys rock! To **Dad and Mom**, thank you from the bottom of my heart for giving me the gift of following my dreams at a young age. To my **friends and family**, I am eternally grateful for all your love, support and laughter; I cherish each and every one of you. To **Jeff Reed**, a special loving thank you; my gratitude for you would take up the entire page, so I really truly thank you for…everything. To **Mason and Maya**, thank you from the depths of my Boogie Bones for being such outrageously awesome kids. I am such a lucky Mom. You are my inspiration, and I love you so much!

Now let's dance! Love, Josie

CREDITS
Created by Josie Bissett
Illustrated by Kevan J. Atteberry
Edited by M.H. Clark and Dan Zadra
Art Direction by Sarah Forster
Designed by Jessica Phoenix and Joanna Price

Library of Congress Control Number: 2011926273

ISBN: 978-1-935414-10-0

Text copyright ©2011 by Josie Bissett
Illustrations copyright ©2011 by Kevan J. Atteberry

1st Printing. Printed in China with soy inks.

For Mason and Maya whose spirits
and smiles light up my life.

~Josie

For my dance partner, Teri. Thanks.

~Kevan

I've come from planet BooGie today.
My mission with you is to DaNce and to play.
I've heard you're a BooGie Monster like me.
You've got your own moves?

...I can't wait to see!

I've traveled the universe **nearby** and **far**,
and I've heard just how **perfectly** special **you** are.
Did you know that nobody else **DANces** the same?
So please take a bow and **tell** me **your** name.

It's so nice to meet you, are you ready to DaNce?
Let's start by imagining ants in our pants.
Then, **wiggle** and **jiggle** your hips, knees, and shins,
and that's just the way that this BooGie begins.

Remember with DaNcing, there's no right or wrong—
you can dance to the music or sing your own song.

You can **shake** all around like a happy wet **dog**,
or roll down a hill like a **runaway log**.

Now here is a move that you might like to try:
pretend you're a helicopter up in the sky.

Just hold out your arms
and start yourself **whirling**

and **spinning** and **soaring**
and **twisting** and **twirling.**

Can you **float** around slowly **like** clouds in the sky, moving **softly** and **gently** as the wind travels by? Can you make a new shape? Can you **glide through the air?** Let the soft breezes **move you** and **rumple** your hair.

There are so many ways that your muscles can work—
you can **wave them** or **shake them** or just go berserk!
The more that you use them, the stronger they'll be,
so won't you get ready to **BooGie** with me?

Can you sit down and dance like you're **riding a bike?**
Spin your legs around **quickly**, that's just what they like!

Imagine you're pedaling **up hills** and **down.**
What things do you see as you're riding around?

Can you dance like a **bear** who is hungry for honey?
Stomp your feet on the floor and start patting your tummy!
Let's show everyone how **fun** it can be
when you let yourself **BOOGie** so perfectly free.

Can you dance like a **robot** with **stiff legs of steel**?
How would you **BooGie** and **how would you feel?**
If your bones and your muscles were all made of **tin**,
show how a robot would **strut, DaNce,** and **spin.**

Can you dance like a penguin who lives in the snow?
Try waddling slowly wherever you go.
It's cool how a penguin can DANCE with no knees.
Get ready to stop, now, when I holler...FREEZE!

With DaNCinG, there's never a wrong way to do it, you do what you please, **and that's all there is to it.** Only you know the way that your DaNCinG should be, so please keep it coming—we'd all like to see!

You can DANCE to the things that you do every day,
make up moves while you're walking, or busy at play.
Try a DANCE like you're eating a plate of spaghetti,
or DANCE like you're throwing some brilliant confetti!

Can you **bounce** all around like a big **kangaroo**?
Keep **hopping**, no **stopping**, whatever you do!
How far can you go in one leaping bound?
How high can you spring with both feet off the ground?

You're beginning to see what this BooGie's about.
You're beginning to figure your own movements out.
What if you danced every morning and night,
and invited some friends to share your delight?

Could we join the whole world in this new kind of DaNce?
Go to Kenya and China and Fiji and France?
Could we all have a party and just dance together?
If we could, I would stay on your planet forever!

Uh-oh...
Planet BooGie is calling, it's time for my snack,
But the next time you're ready, I'd love to come back.
And remember, whenever you've got the chance
To put on your best BooGie LeGS and just DaNce!